SAM'S
Winter Book

WEATHER FARMER BOB ™

visit us at www.flyingrhino.com

EDUCATION ®

Mailing Address: P.O. Box 3989
Portland, Oregon, U.S.A.
97208-3989

E-mail Address: bigfan@flyingrhino.com

Library of Congress Control Number:
99-096719

ISBN 1-883772-22-2
ISBN 1-883772-77-X Farmer Bob Weather series

Printed in Mexico

I am Sam.
I am a ram.

It is winter.

I am cold.

I put on a hat.
I put on my mittens.

9

It snows in the winter on the farm.

Farmer Bob likes to ski.

I like to ride my sled in the winter.

Jenny the Dog likes to ice skate.

17

I am going to make a snow sheep.

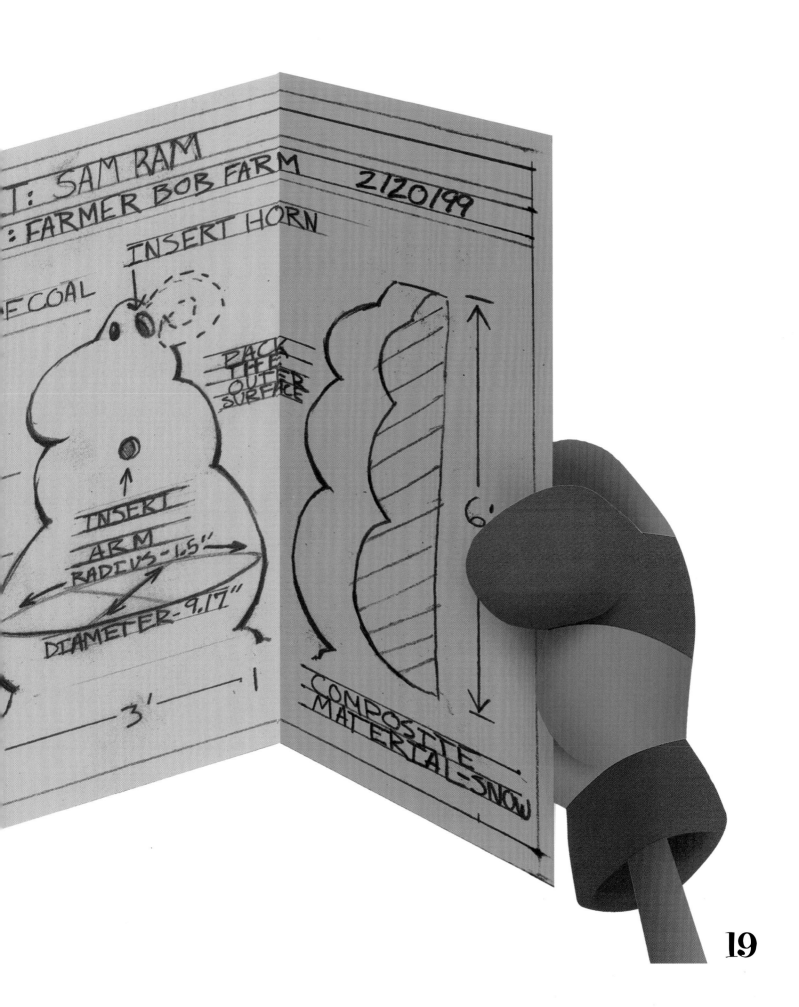

19

I use a big snowball for his body.
I use a smaller snowball for his head.

21

His eyes are two pieces of coal.
I make horns from two sticks.

23

SPLAT!

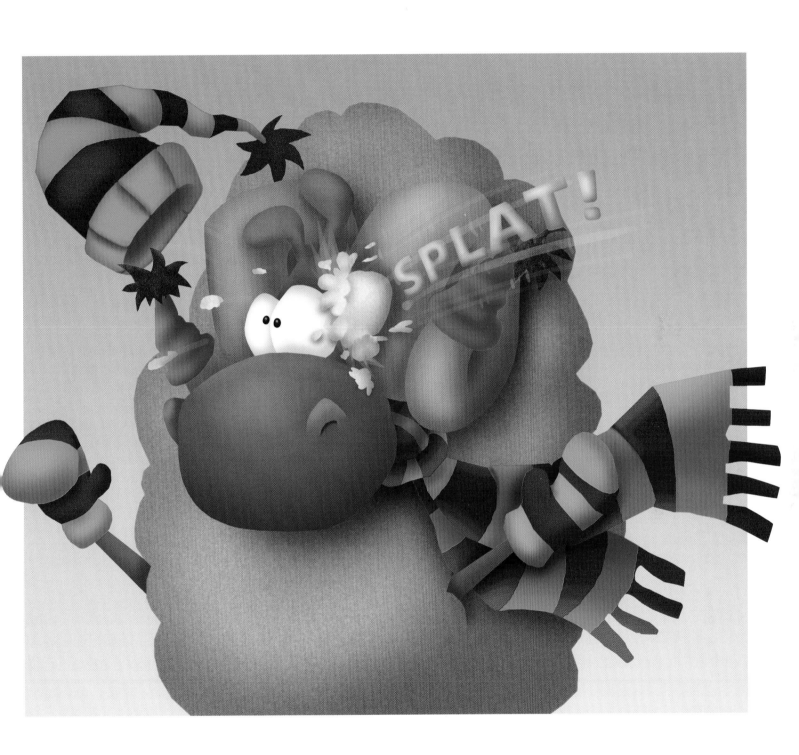

Snowball fight!

When the day is over, we drink hot cocoa.
I love winter.

GLOSSARY

ice skate
(verb)

Sam the Ram and Jenny like to ice skate on the pond.

mittens
(noun)

Mittens keep Sam's hands warm when it is cold outside.

sled
(noun)

Sam the Ram goes down the hill very fast on his sled.

ski
(verb)

Farmer Bob likes to ski in the winter.

snow
(noun)

Sam likes to play in the snow.

ABOUT THE AUTHORS AND ARTISTS

 Ben Adams says farm animals are smelly, but he likes to draw pictures of them anyway. Ben lives in his very own house in Portland, Oregon. He likes to spend time in his backyard pruning, watering, and sculpting his trees into giant farm animals. Someday, he hopes to have his own tree farm and change his name to Farmer Ben.

 Julie Hansen grew up in Tillamook, Oregon, and knows a lot about cows. Although she has never actually owned a cow, she has raised almost everything else: dogs, cats, chickens, rabbits, frogs, rats, mice, fish, ducks, snakes, squirrels, and the occasional muskrat. She lives in Salem, Oregon with her husband, Mark, their son, Chance, two cats, and a dog the size of a cat.

 Kyle Holveck lives in Newberg, Oregon, with his wife, Raydene, and their daughter, Kylie. In Newberg, there are lots of farms and animals. Kyle's favorite farm animal is the rhinoceros, which *we* know is not really a farm animal. Because his house is too small to keep a rhinoceros, Kyle has a chihuahua named Pedro instead.

 Aaron Peeples's hero is Farmer Bob. He says that any man who can look good wearing overalls day after day is definitely a great man. Aaron is currently attending college in Portland, Oregon, and enjoys drawing farm animals at Flying Rhinoceros between classes.

 Ray Nelson thinks cows and pigs are really neat. He also thinks bacon and hamburgers are really neat. (We haven't told him where bacon and hamburgers come from yet.) Ray lives in Wilsonville, Oregon, with his wife, Theresa. They have two children, Alexandria and Zach, and a mutant dog named Molly.

CONTRIBUTORS: Melody Burchyski, Jennii Childs, Paul Diener, Lynnea "Mad Dog" Eagle, MaryBeth Habecker, Mark Hansen, Lee Lagle, Mari McBurney, Mike McLane, Chris Nelson, Hillery Nye, Kari Rasmussen, Steve Sund, and Ranjy Thomas.

visit us online:
www.**flyingrhino**.com
or call 1-800-537-4466